WHERE IN AMERICA IS CARMEN SANDIEGO?

By John Peel

Illustrated by Allan Neuwirth

Additional Coloring by Paul J. Becton

FOR WARREN

—A.N.

A GOLDEN BOOK • NEW YORK

Western Publishing Company, Inc.

Racine, Wisconsin 53404

Alcatraz—once an escape-proof prison—is now a tourist attraction in San Francisco Bay. But one wing has just been reopened, because Alcatraz is the only place in the world that can keep Carmen Sandiego and her gang captive. But wait. What's this? CARMEN AND THE GANG HAVE ESCAPED!

You are now an investigator working for the Acme Detective Agency. The agency chief has just called you into his office. He's giving you the Alcatraz jailbreak case. Memorize these faces. It's your job to track down Carmen Sandiego and her gang. Good luck!

CARMEN SANDIEGO
A tall, natural beauty. Almost always wears a trench coat and fedora hat. Intelligent, sophisticated, and very glamorous. Loves jewelry, especially rubies. Plans thefts no one else would even dare consider. Seems to commit crimes simply for the challenge of doing what others think is impossible.

JUSTIN CASE
Ambulance-chasing lawyer who specializes in personal injury cases. Highly dramatic and can cry on cue in front of any jury. In his mid-40s, with a slight paunch that he tries to hide with a vest.

KEN HARTLEY REED
Muscle-bound oaf who's dumber than a door. Never allowed to participate in the planning phase of a crime. Primary function is to provide brawn and look puzzled if asked anything more complicated than the time of day. Wears Rambo-type clothes and a headband. In his 30s.

KITTY LITTER
Cannot resist stray animals of any size, shape, or description. Generally trailed by a string of cats, dogs, and/or gerbils. Trained a parrot to hide inside any bank and memorize the combination of the bank safe. Suspect is 18 or 19 and wears typical teen clothing: jeans and T-shirts.

WE'VE ESCAPED FROM JAIL, GUMSHOES! WE PLAN TO ROB OUR WAY ACROSS AMERICA AND BACK AGAIN. TRY AND CATCH US. WE DON'T THINK YOU CAN DO IT!
LOVE, Carmen

This is San Francisco, California, a tourist's paradise. Carmen and her gang are up to their old tricks. They're not seeing the sights—they're stealing them! Can you find Carmen, Kitty Litter, Justin Case, and Ken Hartley Reed? Then figure out what each one is stealing.

Carmen is leaving you a special clue each time she appears. If you write down the names of the things she is stealing, a message will become clear.

Some say there are more cars than people in California—especially in Los Angeles. Carmen and her gang are driving cars, too—cars they have "borrowed" from other people. Can you find Carmen, Kitty, Ken, and Justin in their stolen cars?

CITY POUND

WAGON O' WIENERS

SCHOOL

HONK!

Arizona's Grand Canyon has lots to see, but Carmen and her gang only care about what they can steal.

If you're a good detective, you'll see that the objects each gang member steals have something in common. Can you guess what it is?

SOUVENIR CANYON ROCKS 25¢

MILK

Welcome to Abilene, Texas. It used to be one of the wildest towns in the Wild West. It's quieter today, except when Carmen and her gang are in town to steal things! Can you find the gang and their loot?

MARSHAL

WANTED
CARMEN
SANDIEGO

ABILENE
ZOO

In Louisiana people still travel the Mississippi River by steamboat. Carmen and her gang would like to disappear with the boat—but right now they'll take anything they can get their hands on! Can you catch them at it?

Nashville, Tennessee, is called the country music capital of the world. Many famous singers have appeared there. But things *disappear* in Nashville when Carmen and her gang pass through town! Can you find the four ridiculous robbers and figure out what they're taking this time?

It's a tense moment at the Kennedy Space Center in Florida. A space shuttle is almost ready for takeoff. But watch out. Carmen and her gang are at the site, taking off with anything they can! Can you spot them before they blast off for their next robbery?

Washington, D.C., the capital of our country, is the president's home. Sometimes awards are given out at the White House. Carmen will never get an award—but she and her gang might take one! Can you see the sticky-fingered foursome?

Have you figured out what the objects that each gang member is stealing have in common? And what special message is Carmen sending?

SEE THE WHITE HOUSE!

KISS-A-BABY
INFLATABLE
INFANT DOLLS
$1.00

CLICK

CLICK

AWARDS

SECRET SERVICE

People who live in Chicago, Illinois, like to play on Lake Michigan. But Carmen and the others are not here for water sports—they're after more loot! Can you sink their plans by catching them?

TUG-AWAY ZONE

Yellowstone National Park, in Wyoming, Idaho, and Montana, is one of the most beautiful vacation places in the world. But Carmen and her chums aren't taking it easy. They're just taking—everything they can! Get busy, Acme Detective. Protect Yellowstone!

DANGER! NO BERRY PICKING!

DO NOT FEED THE BEARS!

In the state of Washington, Mount Rainier is the headquarters for winter sports. But Carmen and her gang know only *one* sport—stealing! Can you find those coldhearted crooks as they try and slip away with their loot?

ONE WAY

Las Vegas, Nevada, is famous for its gambling casinos. But Carmen and her pals aren't trying to win any games—they're trying to steal them. See if you, Acme Detective, can catch them in the act.

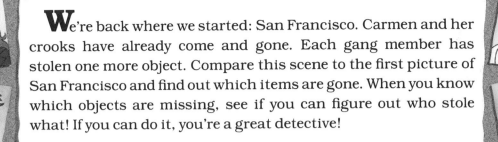

We're back where we started: San Francisco. Carmen and her crooks have already come and gone. Each gang member has stolen one more object. Compare this scene to the first picture of San Francisco and find out which items are gone. When you know which objects are missing, see if you can figure out who stole what! If you can do it, you're a great detective!

WHARFY FUN ARCADE

HOT HU

"O-FISH-AL" SOUVENIRS

WHARF STUFF

YOU GIVE ME A HADDOCK

GOLDEN STATE

A's

At last! Carmen Sandiego, Justin Case, Kitty Litter, and Ken Hartley Reed have been arrested and returned to Alcatraz. Here's a list of all the objects stolen by each character—in every city.

	San Francisco	Los Angeles	Grand Canyon	Abilene	Mississippi River	Nashville	Kennedy Space Center
Carmen Sandiego	crabs	apple car	raft	monkey	elephant painting	note	satellite dish
Ken Hartley Reed	lantern	car	baseball cap	tepee	wallet	cowboy boots	oxygen tank
Justin Case	mannequin	school bus	life preservers	target	cake	wig	model airplane
Kitty Litter	rowboat	truck	donkey	fish	suitcase	guitar	telescope

	Washington, D.C.	New York City	Chicago	Yellowstone National Park	Mount Rainier	Las Vegas	Second visit to San Francisco
Carmen Sandiego	awards	necklace	duckie	ice-cream cone	earmuffs	gambling chips	oyster stand
Ken Hartley Reed	band uniform	books	buoy	blueberries	snowmobile	neon sign	car
Justin Case	kite	statue	yacht	yellow stones	chairlift seat	headdress	bananas
Kitty Litter	dog	horse	catamaran	bear cub	barrel	one-armed bandit	dog

What was similar about the objects each of these people stole? Answer: Everything Carmen stole was red. Everything Kitty Litter stole was brown. Ken Hartley Reed's favorite color was blue. Justin Case preferred yellow.

But what about the second mystery—a separate set of clues left by Carmen herself? Answer: Look at the names of the objects stolen by Carmen. The first letters spell *her* name!

Good work, Acme Detective. But here's one last assignment. Kitty Litter's favorite orange tabby can be found in every picture in the book. Go back to the beginning—and find that cat!